Great I·R·I·S·H Legends for children

Retold by **Yvonne Carroll**

Illustrated by **Robin Lawrie**

PELICAN PUBLISHING COMPANY
GRETNA 2013

Contents

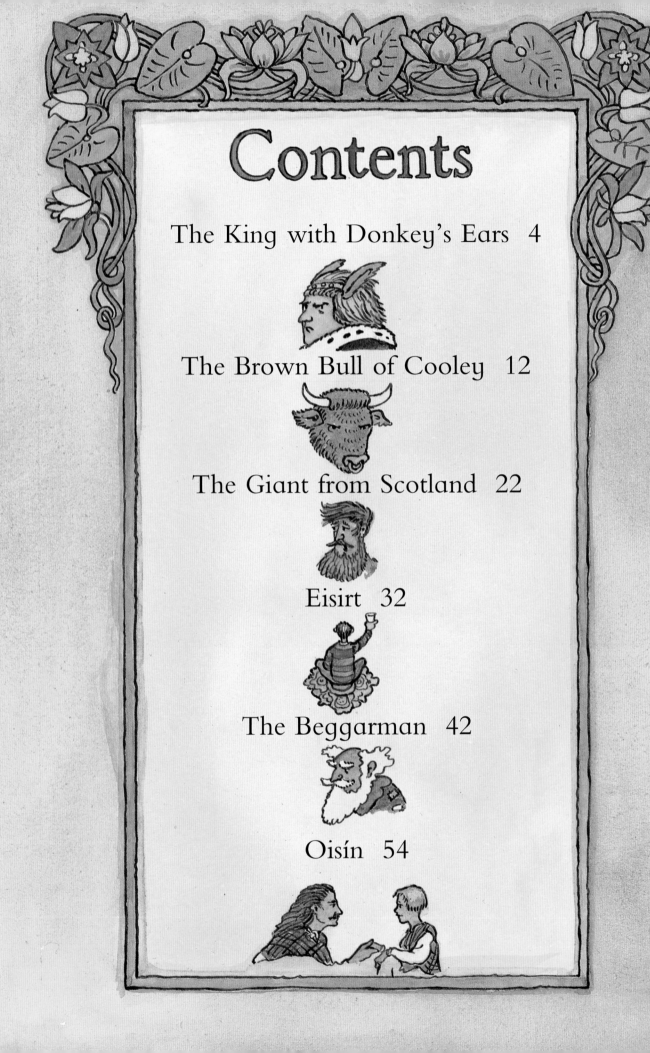

Introduction

This selection of the best-loved Irish legends are enjoyed by children from generation to generation. They have been told for hundreds of years and are part of Irish history.

Fionn builds a causeway of stone all the way to Scotland, while the Fianna meet the most amazing beggarman. A young barber discovers the king's terrible secret, and the army of Ulster are cast under the spell of the sea-witch, leaving only the Red Branch boys to defend the city.

With stories of great giants, clever warriors, jealous queens and mystical creatures, there is something for everyone to enjoy.

To help with reading the unusual names, there is a pronunciation guide on the last page.

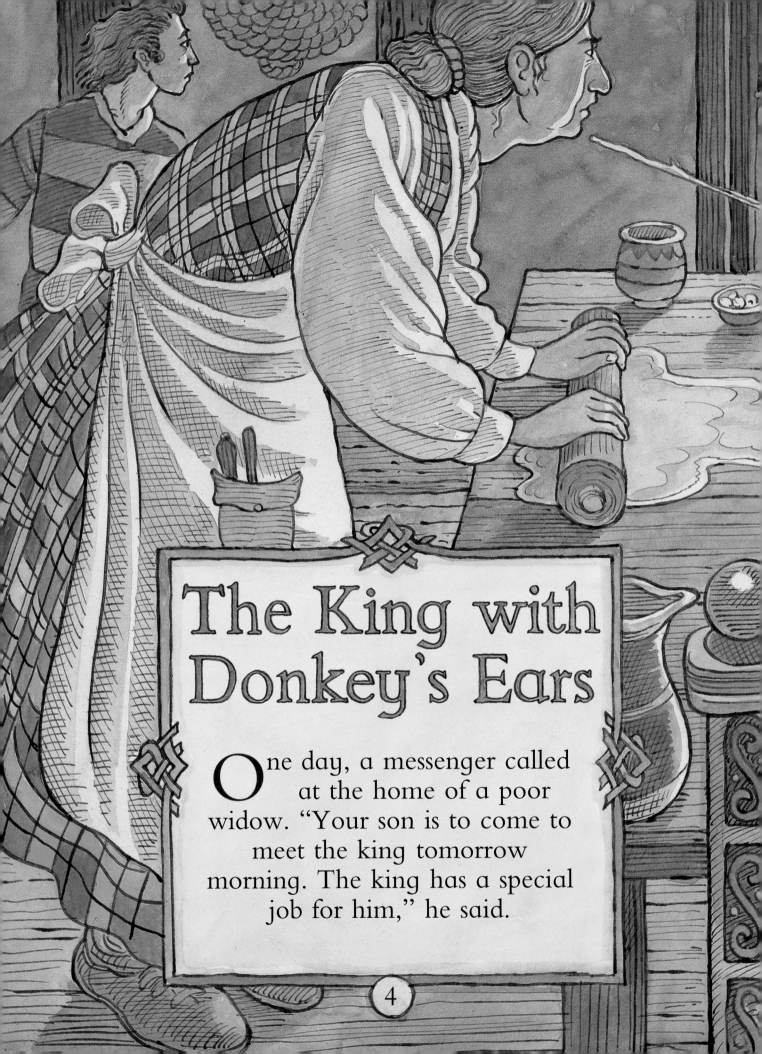

The King with Donkey's Ears

One day, a messenger called at the home of a poor widow. "Your son is to come to meet the king tomorrow morning. The king has a special job for him," he said.

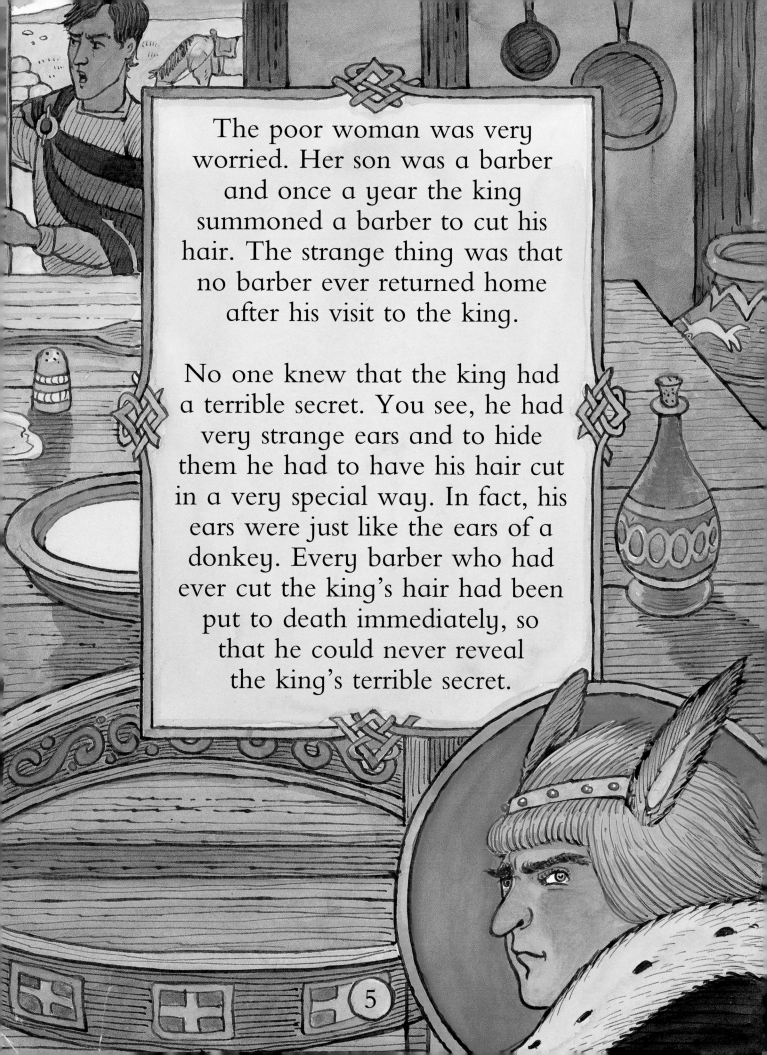

The poor woman was very worried. Her son was a barber and once a year the king summoned a barber to cut his hair. The strange thing was that no barber ever returned home after his visit to the king.

No one knew that the king had a terrible secret. You see, he had very strange ears and to hide them he had to have his hair cut in a very special way. In fact, his ears were just like the ears of a donkey. Every barber who had ever cut the king's hair had been put to death immediately, so that he could never reveal the king's terrible secret.

The woman made her way to see the king. "My son is all that I have in the world," she cried. "Please do not kill my son. If he dies I will have no one to care for me."

The king was sorry for the old woman and he thought for a while. "I will agree to spare his life on one condition," he replied. "Your son must promise never to tell any living person about anything he sees while he is in my castle." Next day the son arrived to cut the king's hair. Imagine his surprise when he saw the king's ears! However, he was a clever boy and he knew that his life depended on his keeping the secret, so he said nothing.

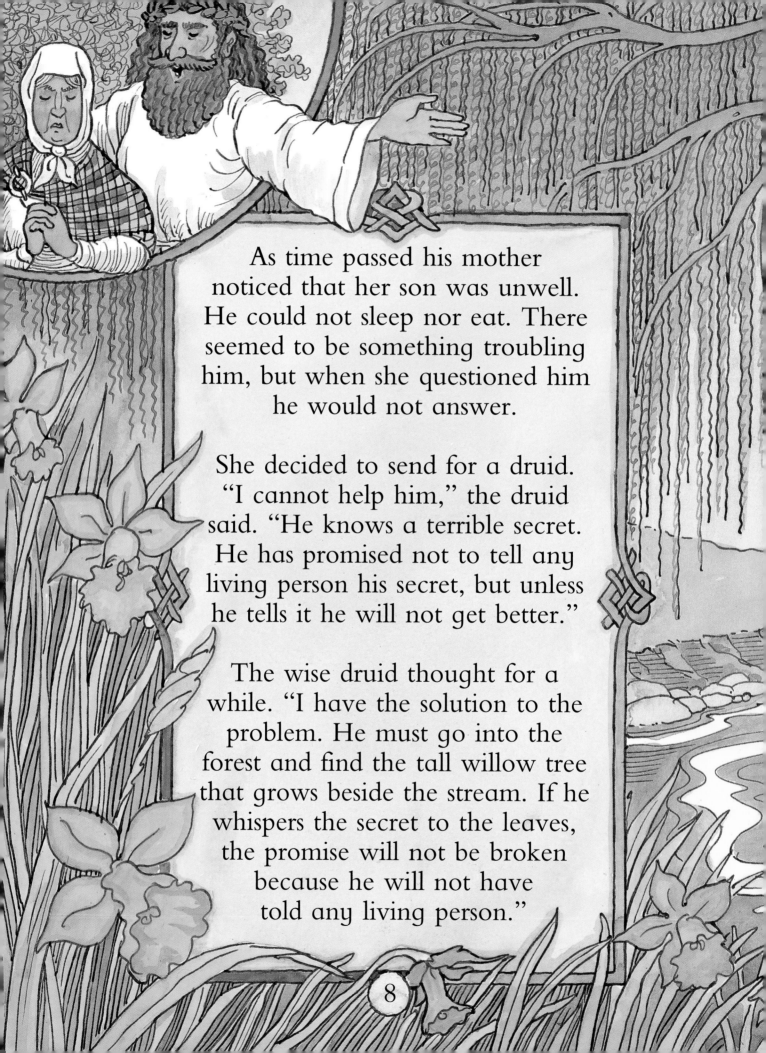

As time passed his mother noticed that her son was unwell. He could not sleep nor eat. There seemed to be something troubling him, but when she questioned him he would not answer.

She decided to send for a druid. "I cannot help him," the druid said. "He knows a terrible secret. He has promised not to tell any living person his secret, but unless he tells it he will not get better."

The wise druid thought for a while. "I have the solution to the problem. He must go into the forest and find the tall willow tree that grows beside the stream. If he whispers the secret to the leaves, the promise will not be broken because he will not have told any living person."

The boy did as he was told and immediately he felt as if a heavy weight was lifted from his shoulders.

That was not the end of the story. Some days later the king's harper went to cut some wood for a new harp.
That night when he began to play for the king and the other chieftains a strange music came from the harp.

"The king, the king, has donkey's ears, has donkey's ears," it sang.

The secret was revealed. At first the king was terrified, but when he saw that no one was afraid of him, or laughed at him, he knew that he would never have to hide his donkey's ears again.

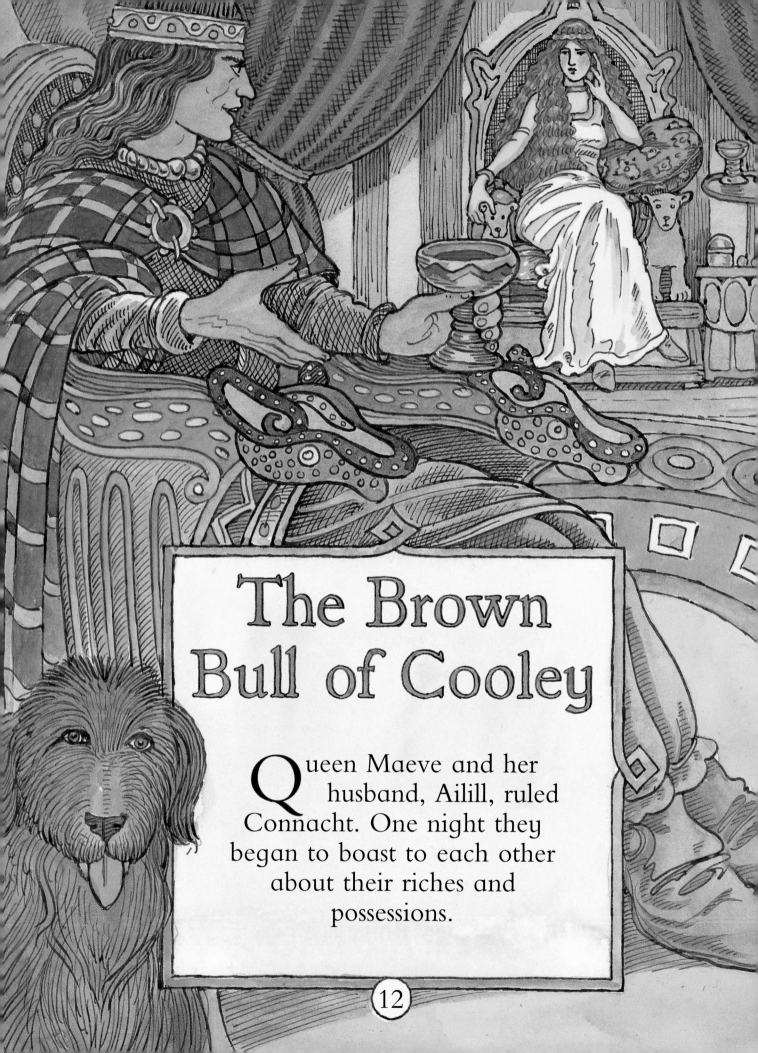

The Brown Bull of Cooley

Queen Maeve and her husband, Ailill, ruled Connacht. One night they began to boast to each other about their riches and possessions.

Maeve had many beautiful jewels, but so had Ailill. Ailill had fine clothes, but so had Maeve. On and on they went, comparing their chariots, flocks of sheep and great herds of cattle. Anything that was mentioned by one was soon matched by the other.

Then Ailill remembered his white bull Finnbhennach. Maeve was silent because she had no bull in her herds like this one.

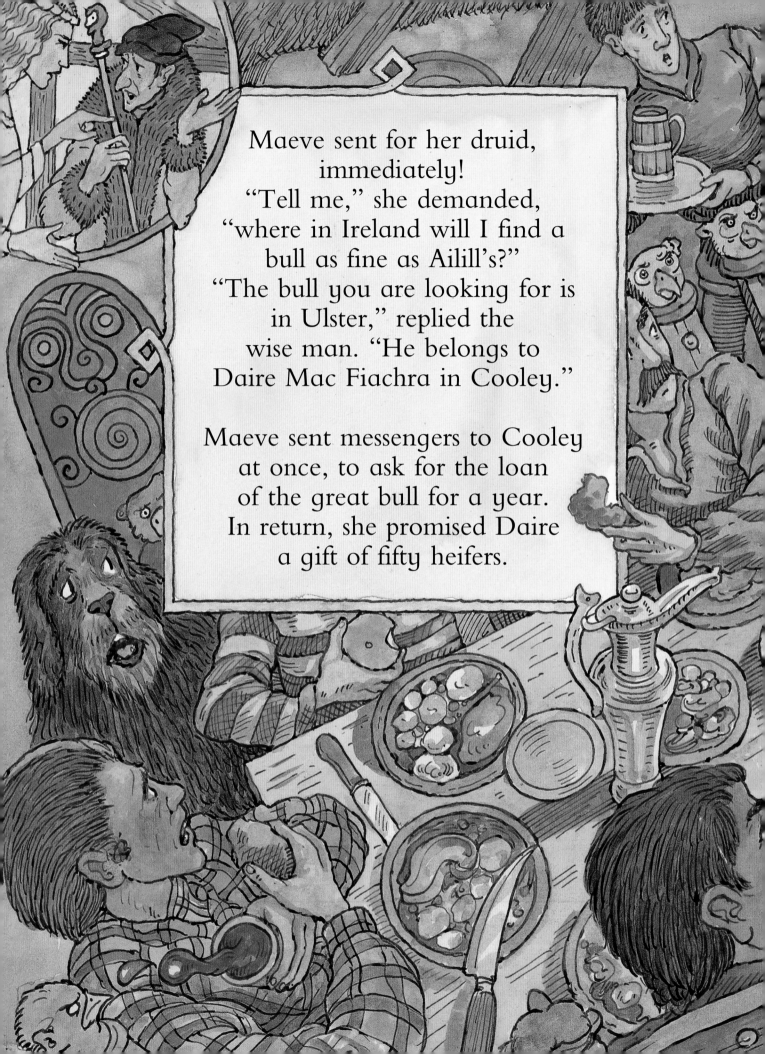

Maeve sent for her druid,
immediately!
"Tell me," she demanded,
"where in Ireland will I find a
bull as fine as Ailill's?"
"The bull you are looking for is
in Ulster," replied the
wise man. "He belongs to
Daire Mac Fiachra in Cooley."

Maeve sent messengers to Cooley
at once, to ask for the loan
of the great bull for a year.
In return, she promised Daire
a gift of fifty heifers.

Daire was delighted to help Maeve and ordered a feast to be prepared for the messengers before they returned to Connacht. During the feast, however, one of the messengers boasted that if Daire had not given the bull willingly they would have taken it by force.

When Daire heard this he was furious. "Return to Connacht and tell your queen that she will not have my bull," he shouted as he sent the messengers on their way.

Maeve was determined to capture the bull. She assembled a great army and marched to Ulster.

It was winter time and during the winter the army of Ulster lay in a deep sleep, under the spell of the sea-witch. When Maeve's army arrived there was only Cú Chulainn and the boys of the

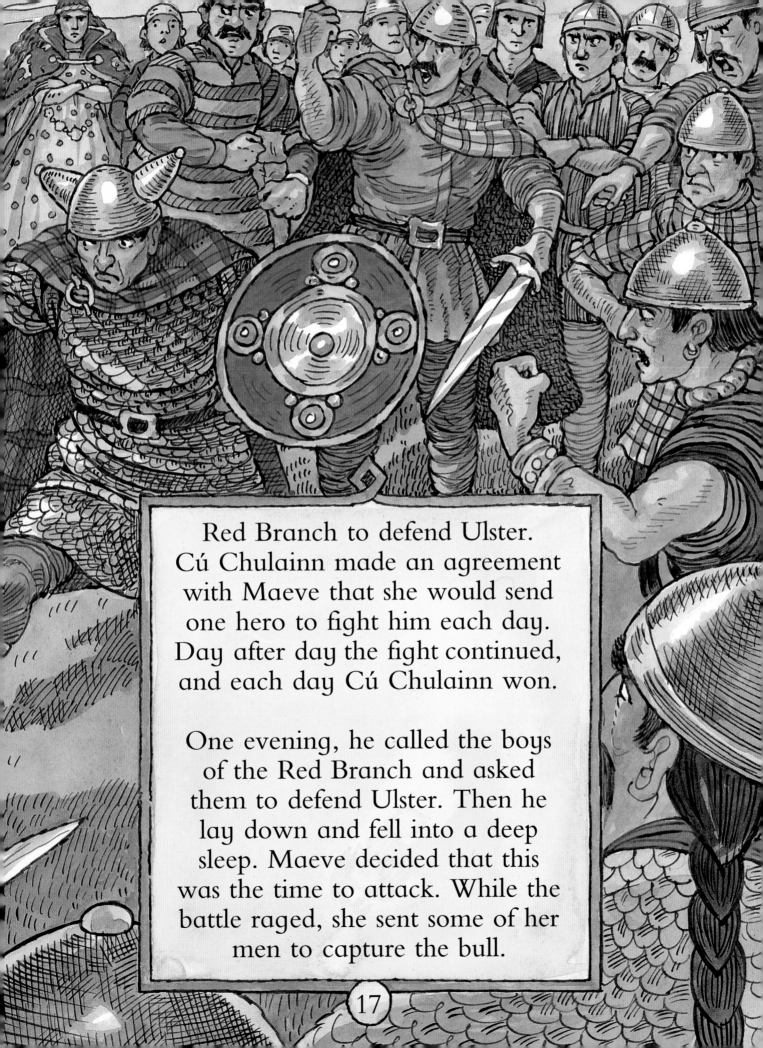

Red Branch to defend Ulster.
Cú Chulainn made an agreement
with Maeve that she would send
one hero to fight him each day.
Day after day the fight continued,
and each day Cú Chulainn won.

One evening, he called the boys
of the Red Branch and asked
them to defend Ulster. Then he
lay down and fell into a deep
sleep. Maeve decided that this
was the time to attack. While the
battle raged, she sent some of her
men to capture the bull.

Cú Chulainn woke to find that most of the Red Branch boys had been killed. By now, spring had returned and the spell of the sea-witch lifted. The men of Ulster rushed to fight but Queen Maeve retreated, driving the huge

brown bull before her.
When she arrived at the castle
she ordered that the bull be put
into a pen to keep him safe.
When Ailill's bull, Finnbhennach,
heard the brown bull bellowing,
it charged. But the brown bull
impaled Finnbhennach on its
horns and the white bull

was killed instantly.
Then the bull turned and, raging
and bellowing, it thundered home
to Cooley. But, no sooner had it
arrived home, than its heart burst
and it collapsed and died. So, in
the end, although a battle had
been fought, neither
Maeve nor Ailill was
richer than the other.

The Giant from Scotland

Fionn and his wife Una lived in their castle by the sea in County Antrim.

One day a stranger arrived. It was a messenger from Scotland, a country across the sea.

"I bring a challenge from the mighty Angus," the messenger said. "He is the tallest, strongest and most fearsome giant in all Scotland. He has heard about your great strength and wants to fight you. Angus has beaten all the other giants and you are the only one remaining. Do you accept the challenge?"

From that day on, Fionn worked
hard. He had decided to build a
path across the sea to Scotland.
It was a rather unusual causeway
made up of hundreds of
thousands of black rocks, all
of different sizes and different
heights. Some rocks had six sides,
some eight and others more
than ten sides.

The warriors of the Fianna
looked on in amazement as
Fionn worked each day. Before
long the causeway stretched
miles into the sea.

24

One evening when Fionn
returned home he noticed
that Una was worried.
"What is the matter?" he asked.
"Oh Fionn," she replied, "I heard
some very disturbing news today.
I heard that Angus is indeed
much bigger than you and that
he is definitely stronger."

"If I cannot beat him with my
strength, then we must think
of a plan. I may not be as
big or as strong as he is, but
I am much cleverer."

Fionn and Una talked for many hours. They thought of many plans, but could not find one that they were sure would work.
Time was running out.
Later that week the messenger from Angus returned and told Fionn that Angus would arrive in two days' time.

"Tell him that Fionn is ready and waiting," said Una.
"Do not worry Fionn, I have a plan in mind."

Una worked hard for the next
two days. She spent the time
cutting and sewing and knitting.
"Imagine sewing and knitting at
a time like this!" he exclaimed.
"I thought you had a plan."

"Look carefully," said Una.
"What do you see?"
Fionn was amazed.
"Clothes," he said. "I see clothes,
but they are most peculiar!"

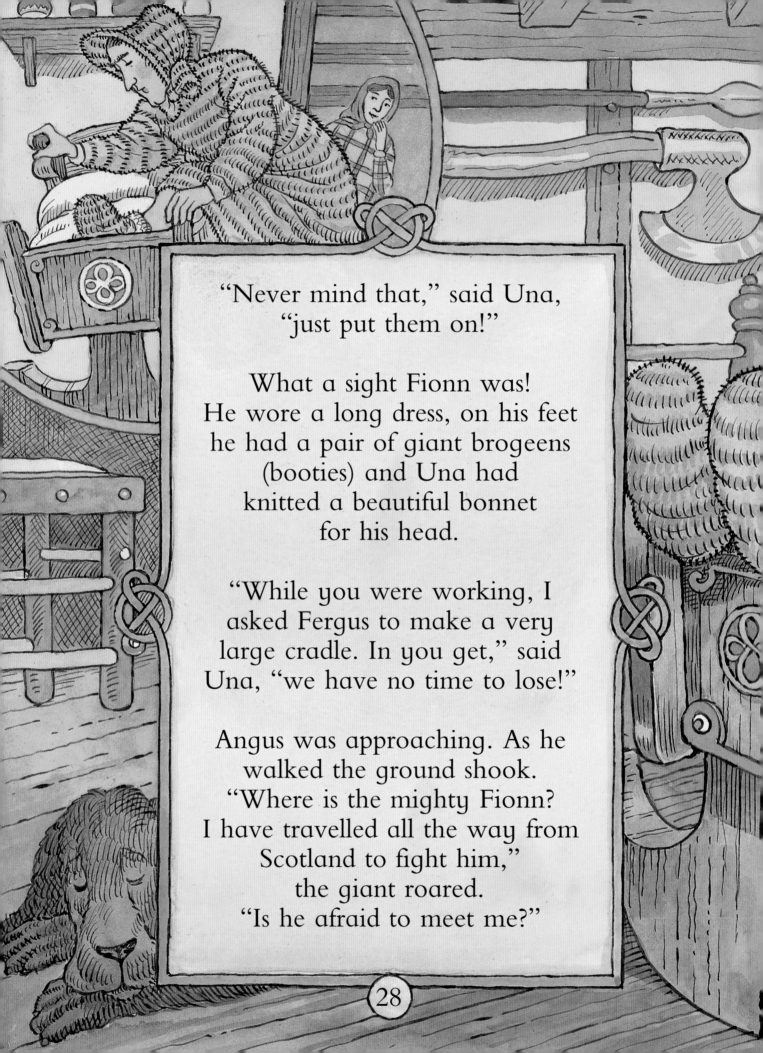

"Never mind that," said Una,
"just put them on!"

What a sight Fionn was!
He wore a long dress, on his feet
he had a pair of giant brogeens
(booties) and Una had
knitted a beautiful bonnet
for his head.

"While you were working, I
asked Fergus to make a very
large cradle. In you get," said
Una, "we have no time to lose!"

Angus was approaching. As he
walked the ground shook.
"Where is the mighty Fionn?
I have travelled all the way from
Scotland to fight him,"
the giant roared.
"Is he afraid to meet me?"

Una opened the door.
"Please come in. You are very
welcome. Fionn is hunting and
won't be very long. But please
sir, could you speak a little softer,
our new baby is asleep."

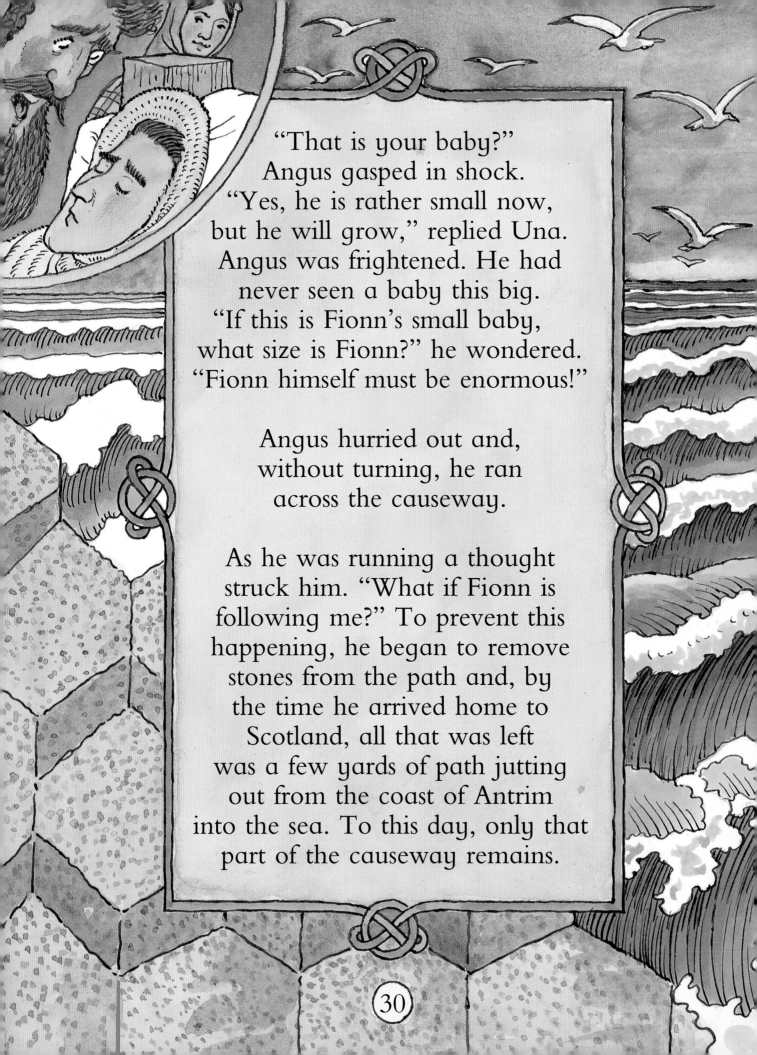

"That is your baby?"
Angus gasped in shock.
"Yes, he is rather small now,
but he will grow," replied Una.
Angus was frightened. He had
never seen a baby this big.
"If this is Fionn's small baby,
what size is Fionn?" he wondered.
"Fionn himself must be enormous!"

Angus hurried out and,
without turning, he ran
across the causeway.

As he was running a thought
struck him. "What if Fionn is
following me?" To prevent this
happening, he began to remove
stones from the path and, by
the time he arrived home to
Scotland, all that was left
was a few yards of path jutting
out from the coast of Antrim
into the sea. To this day, only that
part of the causeway remains.

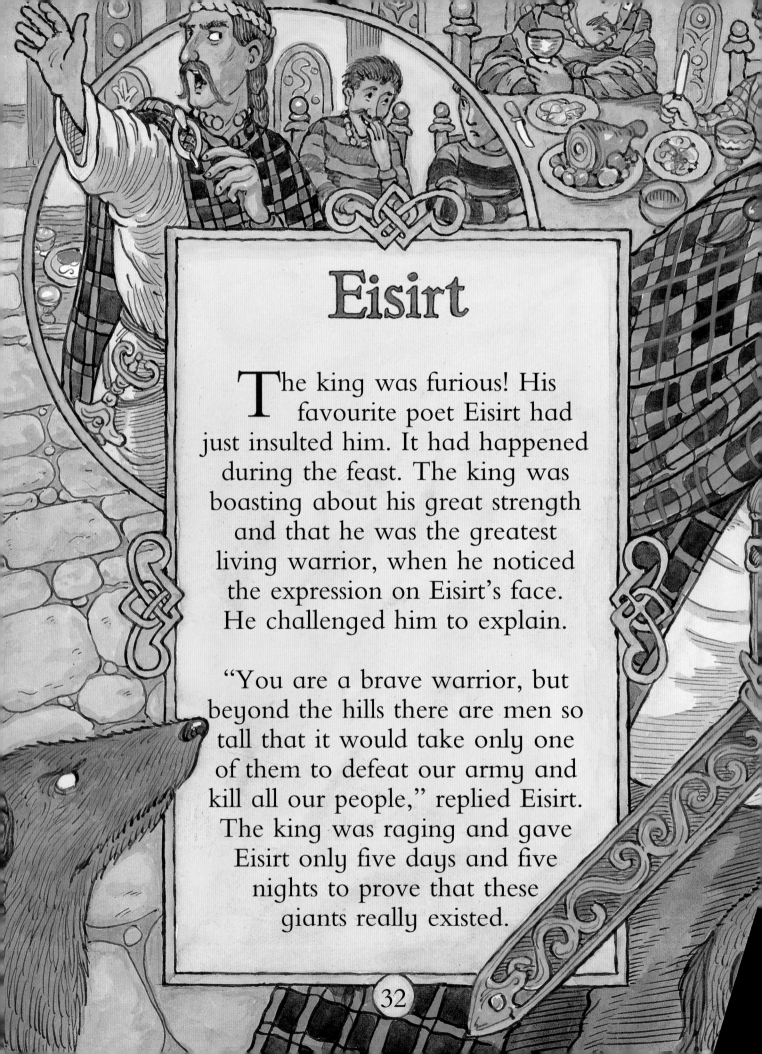

Eisirt

The king was furious! His favourite poet Eisirt had just insulted him. It had happened during the feast. The king was boasting about his great strength and that he was the greatest living warrior, when he noticed the expression on Eisirt's face. He challenged him to explain.

"You are a brave warrior, but beyond the hills there are men so tall that it would take only one of them to defeat our army and kill all our people," replied Eisirt. The king was raging and gave Eisirt only five days and five nights to prove that these giants really existed.

Eisirt set off. He had a problem. If he didn't return with proof, he would be laughed at and would probably be punished. On the other hand, if he found these giants they might kill him.

33

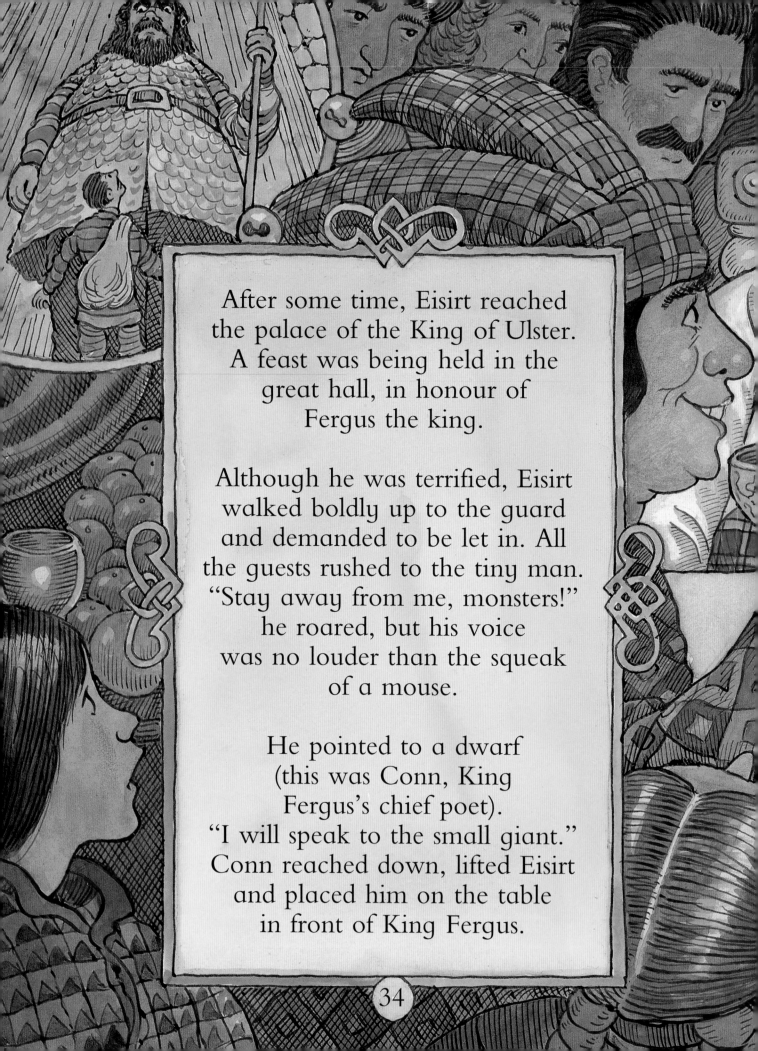

After some time, Eisirt reached
the palace of the King of Ulster.
A feast was being held in the
great hall, in honour of
Fergus the king.

Although he was terrified, Eisirt
walked boldly up to the guard
and demanded to be let in. All
the guests rushed to the tiny man.
"Stay away from me, monsters!"
he roared, but his voice
was no louder than the squeak
of a mouse.

He pointed to a dwarf
(this was Conn, King
Fergus's chief poet).
"I will speak to the small giant."
Conn reached down, lifted Eisirt
and placed him on the table
in front of King Fergus.

34

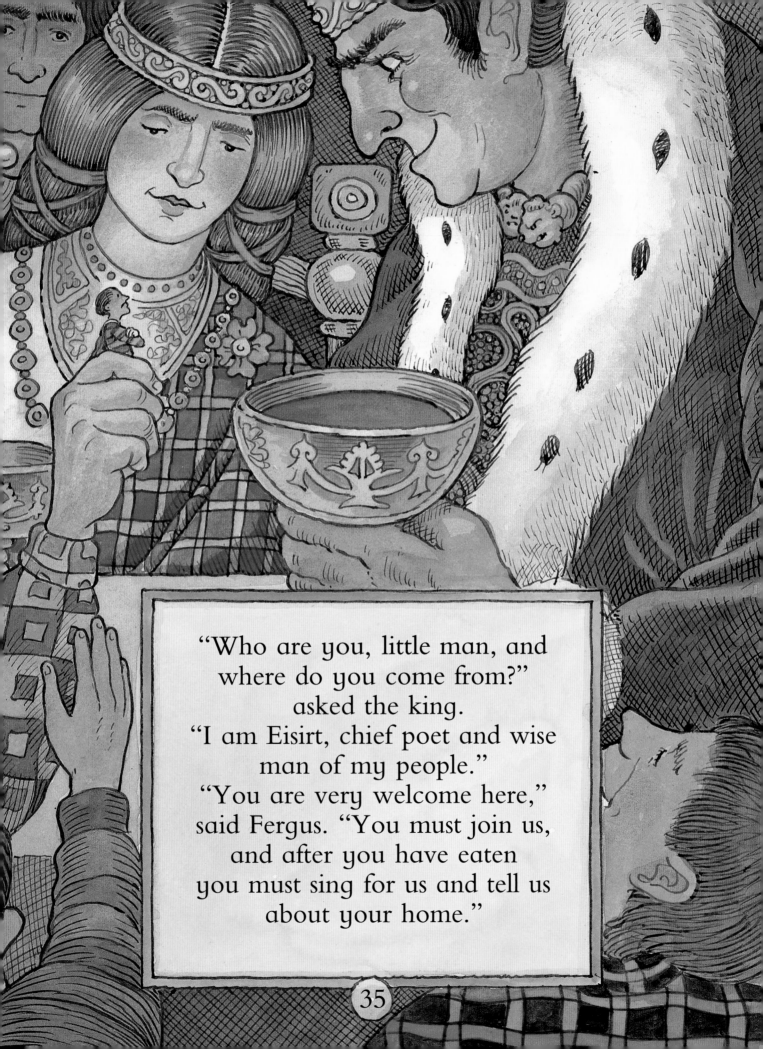

"Who are you, little man, and
where do you come from?"
asked the king.
"I am Eisirt, chief poet and wise
man of my people."
"You are very welcome here,"
said Fergus. "You must join us,
and after you have eaten
you must sing for us and tell us
about your home."

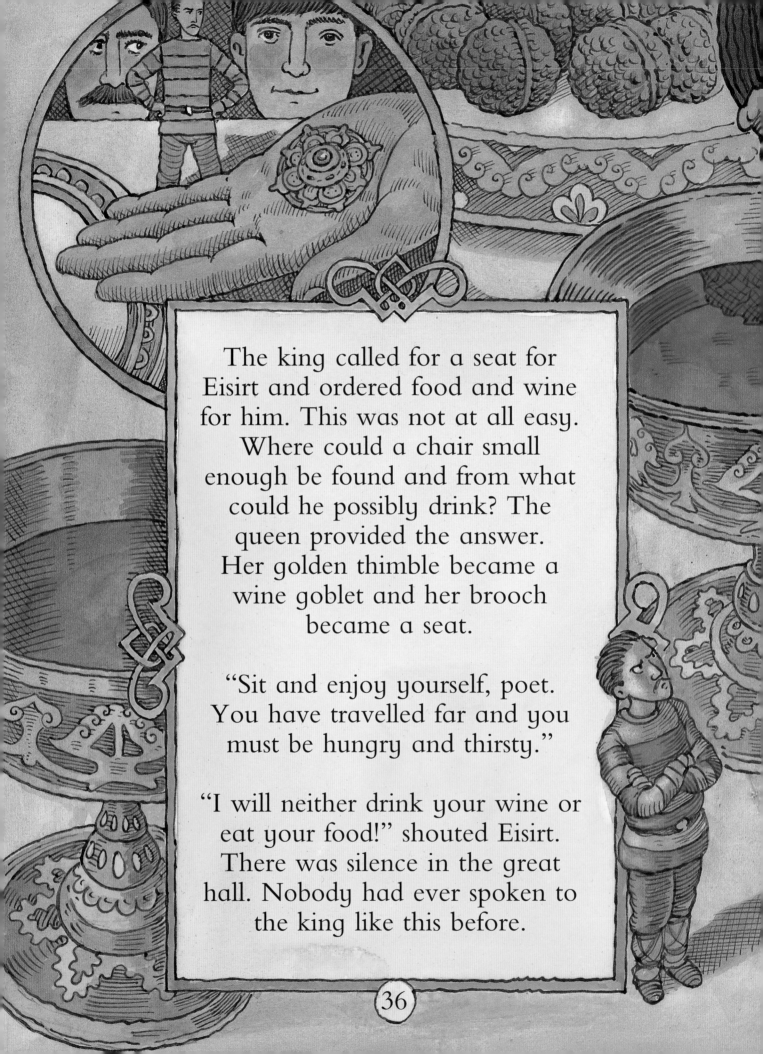

The king called for a seat for Eisirt and ordered food and wine for him. This was not at all easy. Where could a chair small enough be found and from what could he possibly drink? The queen provided the answer. Her golden thimble became a wine goblet and her brooch became a seat.

"Sit and enjoy yourself, poet. You have travelled far and you must be hungry and thirsty."

"I will neither drink your wine or eat your food!" shouted Eisirt. There was silence in the great hall. Nobody had ever spoken to the king like this before.

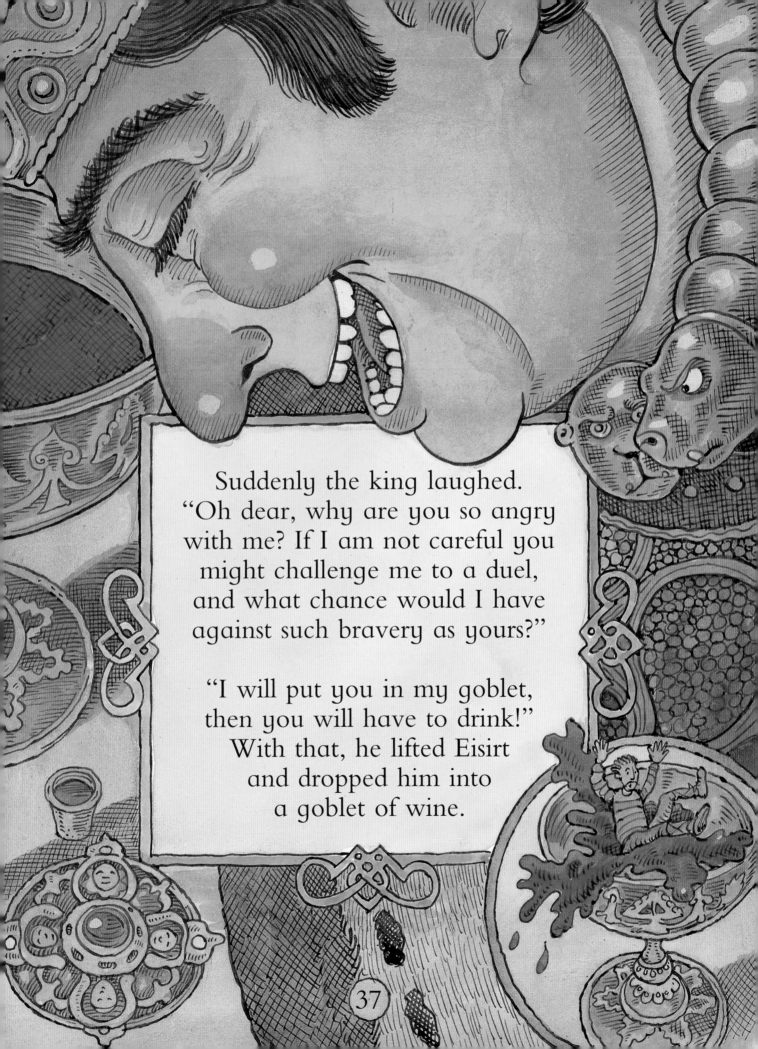

Suddenly the king laughed.
"Oh dear, why are you so angry
with me? If I am not careful you
might challenge me to a duel,
and what chance would I have
against such bravery as yours?"

"I will put you in my goblet,
then you will have to drink!"
With that, he lifted Eisirt
and dropped him into
a goblet of wine.

The little man tried to swim. "King Fergus of Ulster, you are doing a foolish thing. If I drown, you will never hear about my wonderful home or where it is." "Save him! Save him!" the guests cried out. Fergus took him out. "Why did you insult us by refusing our hospitality?" "If I told you," answered Eisirt, "you would be very angry with me. I don't think that people who make you angry live very long."

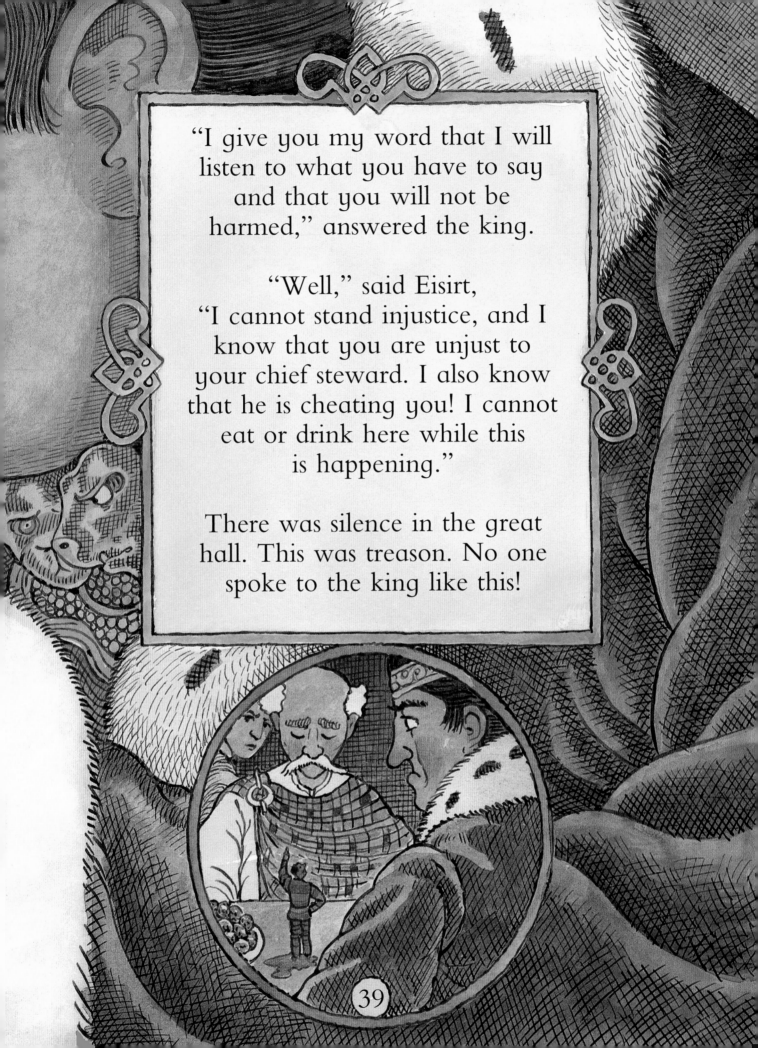

"I give you my word that I will listen to what you have to say and that you will not be harmed," answered the king.

"Well," said Eisirt, "I cannot stand injustice, and I know that you are unjust to your chief steward. I also know that he is cheating you! I cannot eat or drink here while this is happening."

There was silence in the great hall. This was treason. No one spoke to the king like this!

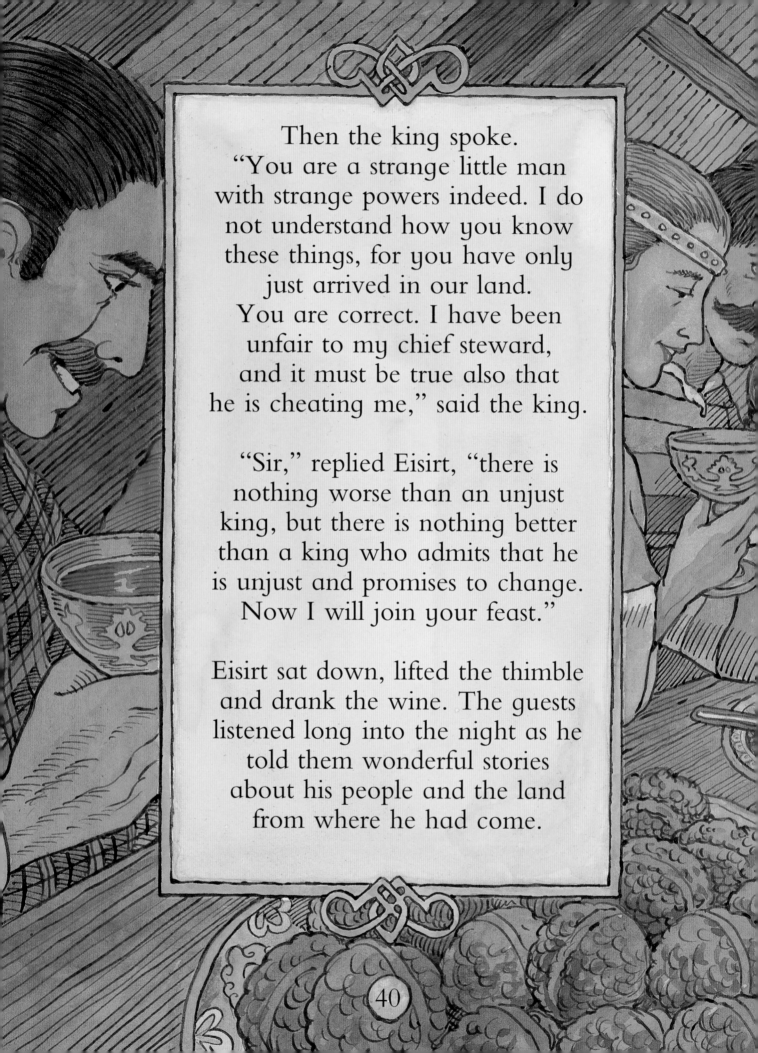

Then the king spoke.
"You are a strange little man
with strange powers indeed. I do
not understand how you know
these things, for you have only
just arrived in our land.
You are correct. I have been
unfair to my chief steward,
and it must be true also that
he is cheating me," said the king.

"Sir," replied Eisirt, "there is
nothing worse than an unjust
king, but there is nothing better
than a king who admits that he
is unjust and promises to change.
Now I will join your feast."

Eisirt sat down, lifted the thimble
and drank the wine. The guests
listened long into the night as he
told them wonderful stories
about his people and the land
from where he had come.

40

The Beggarman

The Fianna were preparing to set out for a day's hunting. They had camped overnight on the Hill of Howth, Binn Éadair.

"This will be a good day," said Conán Maol. "I feel well so I will run fast. In fact, today I will run faster than anyone anywhere!"

All the Fianna laughed, because Conán was short and rather fat. Suddenly, a voice spoke. It seemed to come from a bush nearby.

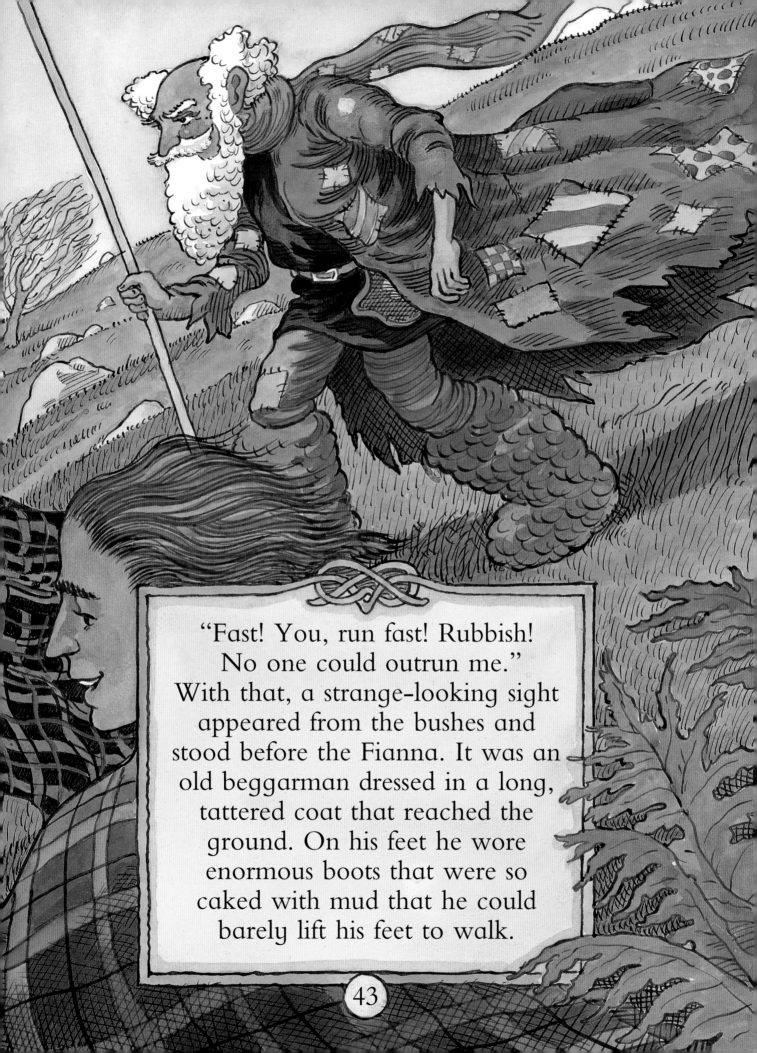

"Fast! You, run fast! Rubbish!
No one could outrun me."
With that, a strange-looking sight
appeared from the bushes and
stood before the Fianna. It was an
old beggarman dressed in a long,
tattered coat that reached the
ground. On his feet he wore
enormous boots that were so
caked with mud that he could
barely lift his feet to walk.

While this was happening, no one noticed a ship sailing into the bay, nor had they noticed the warrior who had jumped ashore and was striding across the beach towards them. As he walked, his golden helmet glistened in the sunlight and his purple cloak blew out behind him.

The Fianna were taken by surprise. "Welcome," said Fionn, leader of the Fianna. But before he could say anything else, the warrior stretched out his arm, pointed to the Fianna and declared, "I offer a challenge. Choose your swiftest runner to race against me. The winner shall have the gold, horses and chariots of Eire."

"Caoilte Mac Rónáin is our fastest runner," replied Fionn, "but he is away in Tara." "The race must take place now!" said the warrior.

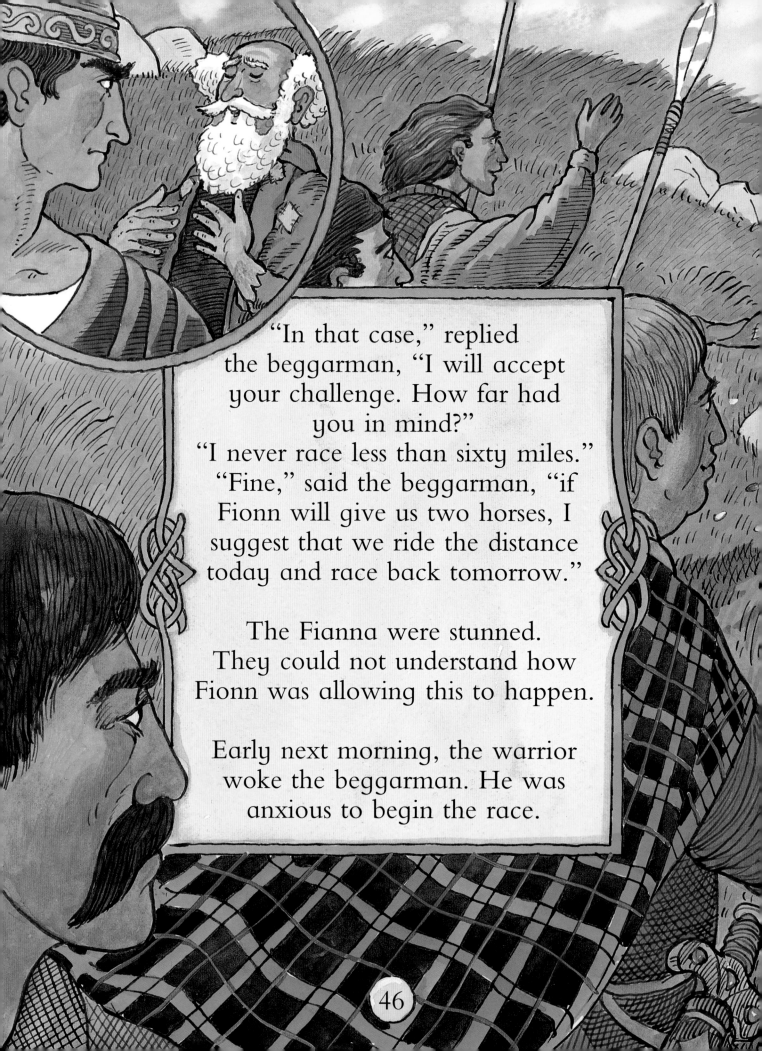

"In that case," replied the beggarman, "I will accept your challenge. How far had you in mind?"

"I never race less than sixty miles."

"Fine," said the beggarman, "if Fionn will give us two horses, I suggest that we ride the distance today and race back tomorrow."

The Fianna were stunned. They could not understand how Fionn was allowing this to happen.

Early next morning, the warrior woke the beggarman. He was anxious to begin the race.

"I would never dream of running this early. If you are in such a rush, you set off and I will follow you later," said the beggarman and, curling up, he fell fast asleep. When he finally woke it was mid-morning. He set off to catch up with the warrior.

What a sight he was, the tails of his long coat flapping in the wind behind him as he jumped and hopped but never ran. But it wasn't long before he had caught up with the warrior.

"We are halfway there now," said the beggarman.
"Have you stopped to eat yet?" There was no answer so he raced on ahead.
"Well, I am hungry and I must eat," he muttered to himself.

The bushes around were thick with ripe, juicy blackberries. The beggarman began to gobble them in fistfuls. By the time the warrior caught up with him, his coat and face were purple with blackberry juice.

"The tails of your coat are caught
up in a bush ten miles back,"
snarled the warrior.
"Oh dear," said the beggarman,
"it would never do for me to lose
them!" Running backwards
he found them, and with three
long hops and a jump caught
up with the warrior again.

Meanwhile, Fionn and the Fianna were waiting on the top of Binn Éadair.
"Do you see anyone coming?" they asked each other.
"I can see something in the distance," whispered Conán Maol.

At the sight of the beggarman the Fianna gave a great cheer of joy and relief. But as they gathered round him, they heard the fearsome roar of the warrior as he approached with his sword drawn. He swung the blade of the sword at the beggarman; but when the Fianna looked, the warrior's head was rolling by the beggarman's side.

"Let that be a lesson to you," said the beggarman. "It's a lucky day for you that I'm feeling generous!"
With that he reached down, picked up the head and threw it back on the warrior's shoulders where it landed back to front!

"Our thanks to you, my friend," said Fionn. "You have saved the honour of the Fianna and I now know who you really are."

Turning to his men Fionn said, "This is the prince from Tír na n-Óg. Once a year he becomes human."
"I have enjoyed my time with you but now I must return to my own people," said the beggarman.

He raised his arms to wave and, as he did, his appearance changed and there before them stood a tall fair-haired prince.

As they watched, a white mist surrounded him and when it cleared he had disappeared, leaving them alone on the Hill of Howth.

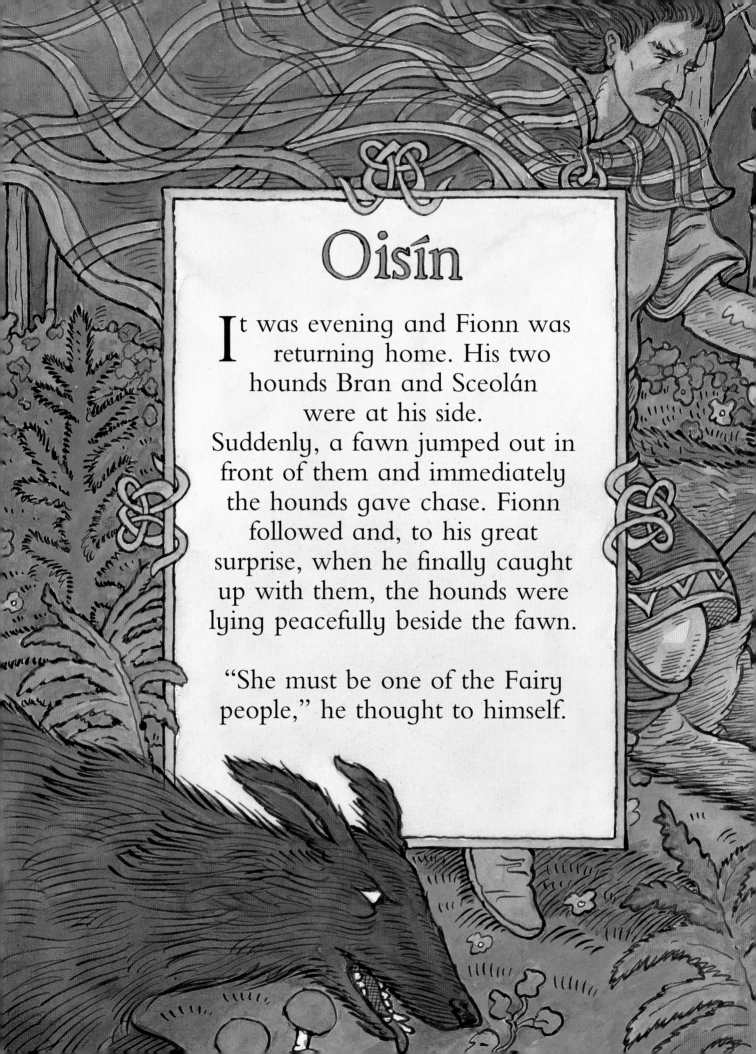

Oisín

It was evening and Fionn was returning home. His two hounds Bran and Sceolán were at his side.
Suddenly, a fawn jumped out in front of them and immediately the hounds gave chase. Fionn followed and, to his great surprise, when he finally caught up with them, the hounds were lying peacefully beside the fawn.

"She must be one of the Fairy people," he thought to himself.

During the night Fionn woke to find a beautiful young girl standing at his bedside. He knew that she must be the fawn he had hunted that day.

"I need your help, Fionn," she whispered softly. "My name is Sadhb, and you are the only one who can help me. Two years ago, one of the druids of my people, the Fear Dorcha, wanted me to be his wife. When I refused, he cast a spell on me and turned me into a fawn. Only the man I love can protect me."

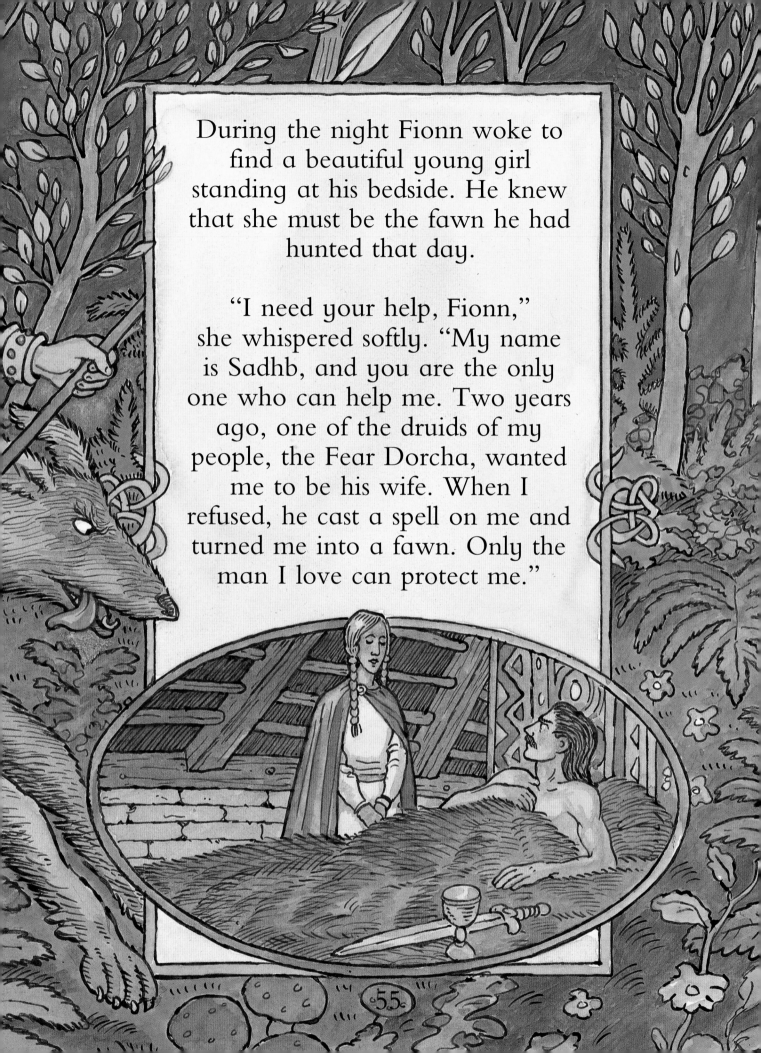

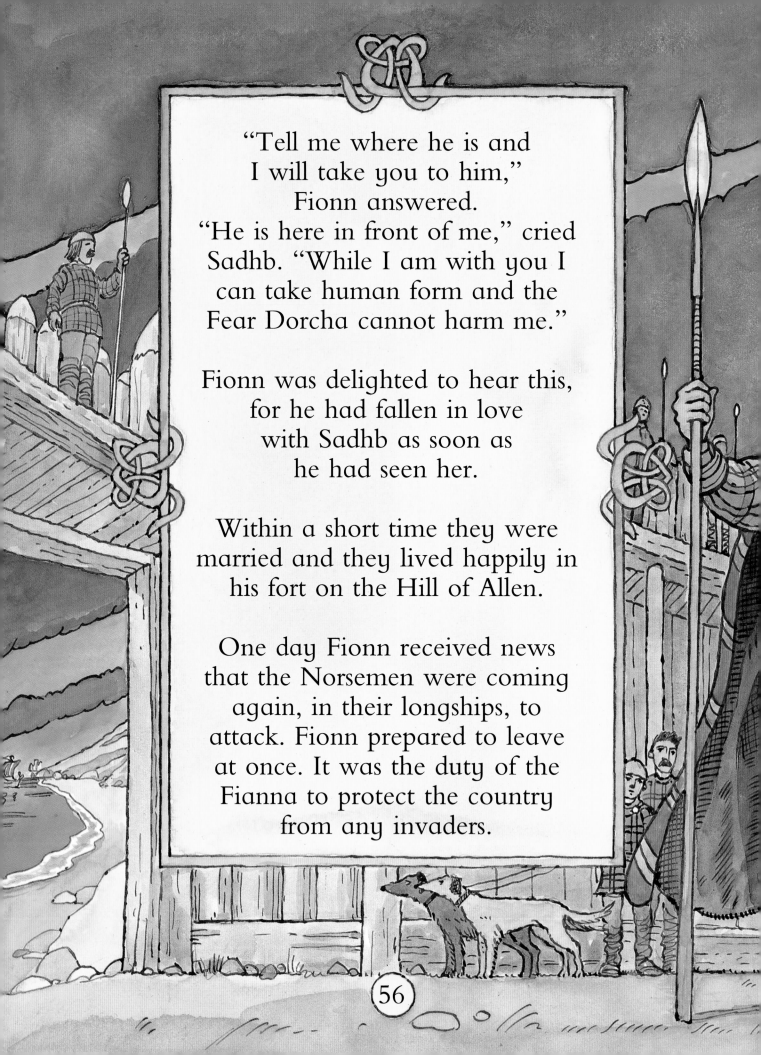

"Tell me where he is and
I will take you to him,"
Fionn answered.
"He is here in front of me," cried
Sadhb. "While I am with you I
can take human form and the
Fear Dorcha cannot harm me."

Fionn was delighted to hear this,
for he had fallen in love
with Sadhb as soon as
he had seen her.

Within a short time they were
married and they lived happily in
his fort on the Hill of Allen.

One day Fionn received news
that the Norsemen were coming
again, in their longships, to
attack. Fionn prepared to leave
at once. It was the duty of the
Fianna to protect the country
from any invaders.

Before leaving he warned Sadhb not to venture outside the fort until he returned. The fight was long and difficult, but eventually the invaders were driven back to their ships. Immediately, Fionn set off for home.

As Fionn approached the fort he was troubled. He could see no sign of Sadhb coming to greet him. Then he grew fearful and rushed into the fort.

His chief steward came to him and told him terrible news. "One morning as Sadhb looked over the plain, she gave a great shout of joy. She cried out that you were returning. We looked out and we saw you with Bran and Sceolán, but were surprised that none of your warriors was with you. Before anyone could say a word, Sadhb ran out to welcome you home."

"As she drew near you, she realised that it wasn't you, but the Fear Dorcha. We were powerless, and could only watch helplessly as he touched her with a hazel rod and she became a fawn. She tried to escape but his two hounds prevented her. There was nothing we could do!"

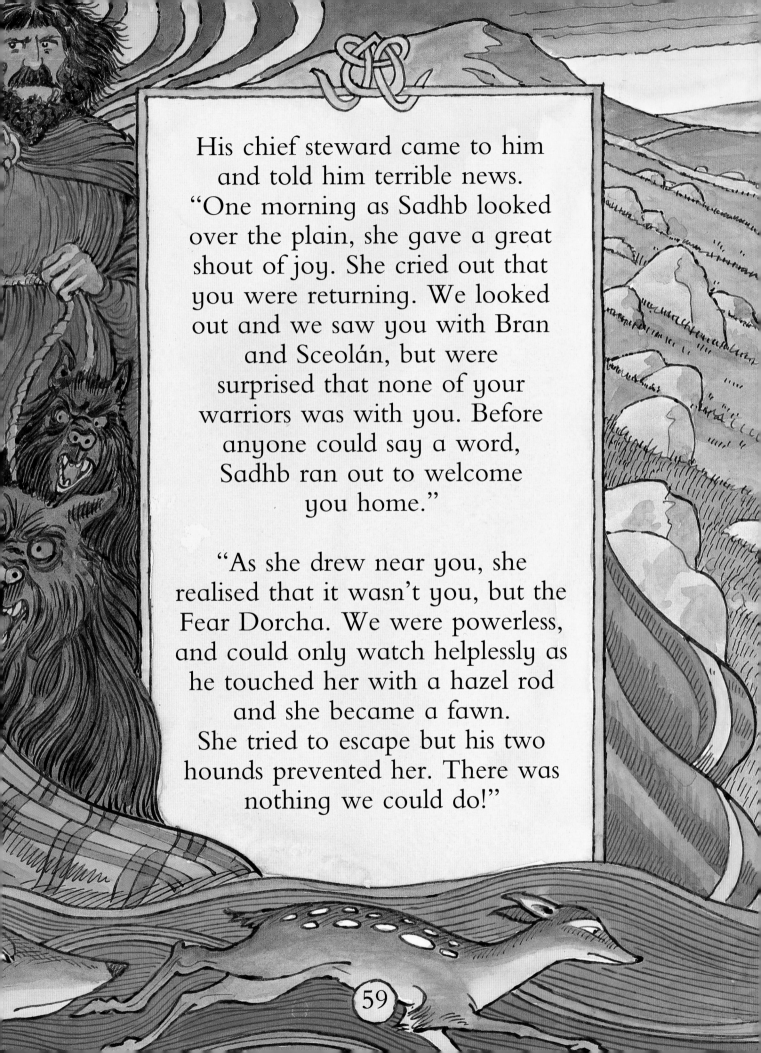

Fionn spent the next seven years searching for Sadhb, but with no success. One evening, as he was returning home, his two hounds suddenly raced off in the direction of a small wood. Fionn was overcome by a strange feeling, and followed them curiously.

There, under a tree, was a little boy of about seven years old. The boy and Fionn looked at each other. Then the little boy reached out his hand and placed it in Fionn's. Fionn looked into the boy's face and recognised the eyes of his beautiful wife, Sadhb. He knew that this was his son.

The little boy returned home with Fionn. At first he could not speak, but gradually, as he learnt the language, he told Fionn about the fawn that had taken care of him.

He spoke about a tall, dark man who would appear and try to talk to the fawn, but she would always run away. The last thing he remembered before meeting Fionn, was the dark man hitting the fawn with a hazel rod and forcing her to follow him.

"You are indeed my son," said Fionn sadly. "I loved your mother, but the Fear Dorcha stole her from me. He has no power over you. You will stay with me and when you are old enough you will join the Fianna. I will call you Oisín, Little Fawn."

Oisín became a great warrior and a famous poet. When he grew up he visited his mother in Tír na n-Óg.

Pronunciation Guide

Ailill
Al-ill

Binn Éadair
Bin Ay-dir

Bran and Sceolán
Bran and
Sk-oh-lawn

Caoilte Mac
Rómáin
Cuill-te Mock
Row-mawn

Conán Maol
Con-awn Mw-ayl

Connacht
Con-ock-t

Cooley
Coo-lee

Cú Chulainn
Cu Cul-in

Daire Mac
Fiachra
Da-ra Mock
Fee-ock-ra

Eisirt
Esh-irt

Fear Dorcha
Far Dr-ka

Fianna
Fee-a-na

Finnbhennach
Fin-van-ock

Hill of Howth
Hill of Hoath

Maeve
May-v

Oisín
Ush-een

Sadhb
Sigh-v

Tír na n-Óg
Tier ne Nogue

Una
Oo-na

Edited by
Helen Burnford & Eveleen Coyle
Designed and illustrated by
Robin Lawrie

Published by Gill & Macmillan, 1994
Published by arrangement in North America by
Pelican Publishing Company, Inc.,
First Pelican edition, 2005
Second printing, 2013

ISBN 9781589803459

Printed in China

Published by Pelican Publishing Company, Inc.
1000 Burmaster Street
Gretna, Louisiana 70053